C0-AVF-342

COP CAMP

EVE BUNTING

Photographs by Richard Hutchings

We would like to extend our thanks to the U.S. Coast Guard Air Station, Floyd Bennett Field, for their assistance.

No part of this publication may be reproduced in whole or in part, or stored in a retrieval system, or transmitted in any form or by any means, electronic, mechanical, photocopying, recording, or otherwise, without written permission of the publisher. For information regarding permission, write to Scholastic Text Division, 730 Broadway, New York, NY 10003.

ISBN 0-590-35190-7

Copyright © 1989, 1977 by Eve Bunting. All rights reserved. Published by Scholastic Inc.

12 11 10 9 8 7 6 5 4   2/9

CHAPTER 1

The motorcycle was parked in front of Joe's Market. Its shiny paint and polished chrome made it glitter in the sun. Andy ran his hand across the seat. It was some bike!

A car came silently around the corner. It was a cop car — black and white with L.A.P.D. on the door: Los Angeles Police Department.

Andy pulled his hand away from the motorcycle fast. Not that he had been doing anything wrong. But you never could tell with cops. Besides, he was Andy Jackson — Skip Jackson's brother. The cop car was stopping.

Andy dug his hands in his pockets and started walking.

"Andy!"

Andy pretended he didn't hear. He kept going.

"Wait up, Andy!"

He didn't look around, but he heard the car door open and close. Andy's heart pounded. He could feel it in his throat.

"What's the hurry, Andy?" It was Officer McGee. He was the cop who had taken Skip in and gotten him sent to Juvenile Hall.

"I didn't do anything," Andy said loudly. "I wasn't going to rip off the bike."

"I know that." McGee dropped his hand on Andy's shoulder. "I've been looking for you."

Andy wanted to push the hand away. "What do you want me for?" he asked.

McGee stopped walking. Because of the hand, Andy had to stop too.

McGee was smiling down at him. "What are you going to do this summer?" McGee's eyes crinkled when he smiled. He had a dimple in his cheek. He seemed young for a cop.

"I don't know," Andy said. "Why?"

"Are you going to camp or anything?"

Andy shook his head. McGee should know he wouldn't be going to camp. Camps cost money.

"I've been looking for a job," he said.

McGee grinned. "There's not much going for 11-year-olds, I hear."

"I'm walking two dogs," Andy said. "Besides, I'm not 11. I'm 12."

McGee took off his cap and scratched his head.

Andy wished he could hate McGee . . . because of Skip. But it was hard. He had always thought McGee was OK, before. McGee never gave him a hard time for skateboarding in the street. He didn't hassle kids for playing ball in the street, either. Andy had to keep telling himself that McGee wasn't what he seemed.

"You want to come to our camp?" McGee asked.

"What camp is that?"

"Police camp," McGee said.

Andy looked at him. "What are you talking about? I'm not in the police."

"The police run it," McGee said. "It's for kids. Kids who can't go to Y camp or places like that."

"Cop camp," Andy said. "Any kid would have to be crazy to go there."

"It's over on the island," McGee said. "We've got tents. We're going to do some snorkeling. Cliff climbing too. Have you ever climbed?"

"Naw," Andy said. "I couldn't go anyway. Mom

needs me at home." He almost said, *now that Skip's gone*, but he didn't. He figured McGee knew the reason.

"I talked to your mom. She said it was OK if you wanted to go. It doesn't cost anything."

Andy shook his head. "No thanks," he said.

"Well, if you change your mind, let me know," McGee said. "We have one place left. I've been saving it for you."

"Are you trying to make up for what you did to Skip?" Andy asked. "No dumb camp could do that." The words came out of his mouth unexpectedly. And his voice sounded funny, as if he was going to cry.

McGee stepped back. "I'm not trying to make up for anything," he said. "Skip got what was coming to him. He stole that old lady's purse. You know that wasn't the first old lady's purse, either. Skip got a lot of warnings."

"Sure," Andy said. "That's what you say!"

"Think about camp," McGee said. "I'll keep that place till tomorrow. I'd really like to have you come, Andy."

"Well, I won't be going," Andy said. He walked off along the sidewalk.

Kids he knew were throwing a ball around in the empty lot. It was too hot for playing ball. It was too hot for anything. He thought about the island. There would be swimming. He wondered what snorkeling was like. The fish would be all

different colors. Too bad it was McGee's camp. Skip would have a fit if he went. And Tug! Tug would laugh at him. "Cop camp," he'd say. "You've got to be kidding!"

He would go talk to Tug. They would laugh about McGee together. He knew he would feel better after he talked to Tug.

CHAPTER 2

Tug was 14, two years older than Andy. They were best friends. Andy knew his mom didn't like Tug. But Tug was fun to be with. He was always thinking up neat things to do. Usually they were not really bad things. But some were what Andy's mom called "on the border."

Once Tug threw a firecracker through an old guy's window. The cops had been mad. "He could have had a heart attack," they said. "But he didn't," Tug said. "He was in another room."

Andy's mom worried that some day Tug would get into bad trouble. She worried that Andy would be with him. "Skip was like Tug to start with," she said. "I've cried over one son. I don't want to cry over my other one."

But Tug wasn't what Andy's mom thought. Tug was OK. Skip liked him too.

Tug was sitting on the steps of his building. He was drinking cherry soda and eating cookies.

"Guess what?" Andy asked.

"I know what," Tug said. "You're going to McGee's camp."

Andy stared. "No, I'm not. Do you think I'd go to that?"

Now it was Tug's turn to stare. "You're not? I am."

Andy eased himself down on the step. It was sizzling hot. "You're going?"

"Sure." Tug crumpled the empty soda can. "It's free. Anything would be better than here. It seems like my mom is never off my back these days. 'Do this, Tug. Do that, Tug.' I wish camp would last a month. A year, even."

"But you hate cops," Andy said. "And you hate McGee most of all, because of what he did to Skip. You said so."

Tug licked the frosting off a cookie. "Who said you have to like McGee to go? If anybody's giving, I'm taking. I'm not fussy." He leaned back on his elbows. "Once I get over there, though, those cops had better look out."

"What are you going to do, Tug?"

"I'll have to check it out first. Too bad you aren't coming."

Andy shrugged.

"You know why the cops are running the camp?" Tug asked.

Andy shook his head.

"So the boys and the cops can get to know each other better. Isn't that sweet?"

Andy knew Tug was watching him closely.

"It's also for problem boys," Tug added. Andy felt his face burning up. Problem boys! He wasn't a problem boy. He had never been in trouble in his life. Sure! It was because of Skip. The cops thought he was the same way. McGee and all his smiles. McGee and his "I'd really like to have you come, Andy."

"Too bad you're not coming," Tug said again. "We sure could have had fun. Maybe not the kind the cops had in mind, but . . ."

"I can go if I want to," Andy muttered. "McGee said so."

Tug uncurled himself and stood. "Well, go tell him, man!" He grabbed Andy's arms and hauled him up. "We'll liven up that camp for them. If they want problem boys, we'll give them problem boys."

"I'll have to find someone to walk the dogs," Andy said.

"Sure, sure." Tug's voice urged him on. "You can do that later. Go tell McGee." Andy could feel Tug's eyes on his back as he walked away.

The station house was only a few blocks away. The guy at the front desk called McGee on a phone. He came running down some stairs.

"I changed my mind," Andy said.

"Hey, that's great!" McGee went rushing around, getting lists of things for Andy. "Also, here's a form your mom has to sign," he said.

Andy put the papers in his pocket.

"How come you decided to come after all?" McGee asked.

"Tug's going." Andy looked straight at McGee's face. The face changed a little. The eyes narrowed. Suddenly it was a real honest-to-goodness cop face. Andy could tell that McGee didn't like Tug any more than his mom did.

"That's right. Tug's a friend of yours."

Andy nodded.

"Well, I'm glad you're coming." McGee stuck out his hand. "It's next Sunday, then, Andy. We'll be by your house to pick you up. Seven a.m."

McGee had come by to pick up Skip too. That had been at night. And Skip hadn't been expecting him. Andy bent to tie his shoelace. It didn't need tying, but that way he didn't have to take McGee's hand.

"See you," McGee said.

"See you," Andy muttered. He let the station door slam behind him.

What was it Tug had said? "If they want problem boys, we'll give them problem boys."

Of course, they wouldn't be real problems, just borderline ones, as Mom would say. Something to shake that cop camp up a little.

CHAPTER 3

They went across to the island in a power boat. It had a crew of two.

"A banker named Saunders lets us use the boat," McGee explained.

"He sure is getting himself in good with the cops," Tug sneered.

"Maybe he just likes kids," McGee said coldly.

Andy counted 15 boys. He looked at them carefully. They all looked OK to him. If they had problems, they were hiding them well.

There were two cops besides McGee. One had a long, funny-sounding name that nobody could pronounce. "Call me Charlie-O," he said. The other's name was Fergus.

Fergus said the island was about two hours from the mainland.

Andy turned his face to the breeze. It felt so cool and clean. He sat on his sleeping bag by the bow.

Tug prowled around the boat.

"Down below is off-limits, Tug," McGee called.

"You told me already," Tug said.

Andy leaned forward, willing the boat to go faster.

At first, the island was just a haze floating in the distance. Then he could see the cliffs.

McGee leaned on the bow rail. "There she is," he said. His voice seemed to sing.

Andy stood up. The island had a rugged look.

It was as though no one had ever set foot on it.

"People live here, don't they?" Andy asked. He was mad at himself as soon as he spoke. He had made up his mind not to talk to McGee unless he had to.

"Not on this side," McGee said. "There's a town clear across the island. But that's 15 miles away. Here it's just the sheep, wild goats, and us."

Andy saw that Tug was back. Tug's eyes were bright with excitement. Andy had seen him look like that before. It was after he'd pulled off one of his "borderlines."

"What's going on, Tug?" he whispered, but Tug didn't answer.

"Grab your stuff, kids," Charlie-O yelled. "We're here."

The power boat dropped anchor. One of the crew lowered a dinghy with an outboard motor. McGee ferried boys and supplies back and forth.

Soon the beach was covered with tents, sleeping bags, and other gear. At noon the big boat pulled away. The dinghy was left behind.

"Mr. Saunders lets us keep it," Fergus said. "We use it to get to the reef for snorkeling."

"Be back for you in a week," one of the crewmen yelled from the boat.

McGee pointed to the top of the cliff. "That's where we'll set up camp," he said. "Start hauling."

Andy walked behind Tug up the narrow path. Now and then he stopped to look down at the sea. It was shining like glass. *A whole week,* he said to himself. *I can put up with anything for this . . . even McGee.*

After they got the tents up, Fergus called them all together. "We're here to have fun," he said. "That's the main thing. But we do have

some rules. First off, stay close to camp. It's wilderness out there. No one goes in the water, climbs, or hikes without asking McGee, Charlie-O, or me."

Everyone nodded.

"Now," Fergus said. "We have six tents and 18 people. That's three to a tent. If you think I'm sleeping with Fergus or Charlie-O, you're crazy." He grinned. "Three tents get a cop."

There were moans and groans all around.

"With my luck . . . ," Tug whispered.

"As long as it's not McGee," Andy said.

It was McGee. Their three sleeping bags lay side by side in the same tent.

"Do cops snore?" Tug said loudly to Andy.

"You'll have a chance to find out," McGee said. "Right now, let's see how the water feels."

The water felt great. It washed away the memory of city heat.

Andy floated on his back. He felt that he was looking at the sky for the first time. It was so blue and there was so much of it.

There was a splashing close to him. Then he heard a soft, gurgly scream. He rolled over.

Tug was pushing a kid's head under the water. He'd shove him down, let him up for a second, then push him under again.

Tug turned a laughing face to Andy. "The crazy kid tries to yell every time he comes up. He should breathe instead."

"Hey!" Andy grabbed Tug's arm. "Cut that out, Tug." The kid's head bobbed up.

A whistle blew, high and loud. McGee's voice came across the water. "You two . . . Tug and Andy. Out of there right now."

"Oh, man!" Tug said.

"You OK?" Andy asked the kid. It was Peewee Peters. Peewee was nine, the youngest kid in camp.

Peewee nodded. He coughed up some sea water and glared at Tug.

The whistle blew again. "I said *out,*" McGee yelled.

Tug and Andy splashed toward shore.

McGee's face was grim. "Don't pull anything like that again or you're through swimming." He pushed past them, heading for Peewee.

"But Officer McGee! You didn't say we couldn't dunk each other. That wasn't in your rules." Tug grinned at McGee's back.

Andy felt a dull kind of anger. *He* hadn't done anything. Wasn't that just like a cop? They never gave you a chance to explain. He was mad at Tug too. "What did you do back on the boat?" he asked angrily. "I know you did something."

Tug's face closed. "I didn't do anything on the boat. You just shut up about that."

Oh, yes, you did, Andy thought. *And it was something bad.* The words rang like a warning bell in his head. *Something really bad.*

CHAPTER 4

They ate dinner early that night. Afterward they sat on the beach around a campfire. Charlie-O told a spooky story. It was about a monster who lived on the island. This monster ate sheep. After he ate their insides, he hung their wooly skins on the trees to drip.

"A tree just like that one over there," Charlie-O whispered.

They were all haw-hawing and nudging each other. But at times their eyes looked into the dark beyond the fire.

Andy didn't notice when Tug slipped away. He just turned and found he was gone. What was he doing, sneaking around in the dark? For a minute Andy wished Tug weren't at the camp. It was scary wondering what he was up to all the time. Back home, it was kind of exciting. It took away the boredom. But here, who needed it?

He glanced across the campfire at McGee. McGee lay back on one elbow. He stretched contentedly.

Andy stared. Skip used to stretch like that. How could he have forgotten Skip, and where Skip was, and who had put him away? Whose side was he on, anyway — Skip and Tug's, or McGee's?

Andy eased himself back from the fire.

"Sometimes the sheep hear the monster coming," Charlie-O whispered. "They cry because they know he's coming and they can't stop him. Sometimes at night you can hear them cry." Charlie-O tilted his head. "Listen! Everybody listen now! Hear anything?"

Andy crept away. It was dark past the fire's glow. He wished Charlie-O hadn't told that story about the sheep. He held his breath, listening. Then, "Don't be a dope!" he told himself. "That was just a kid's story. Nothing to worry about."

But where was Tug?

A thin finger of light came from behind a large rock. Andy narrowed his eyes. There was a shadow too. Tug was crouched, bent over the sand. What was he doing? Andy moved soundlessly forward. He made himself small as he ran. Now he was close enough to see. Tug had dug a hole. He was burying something.

"Tug?" Andy whispered.

Tug swung around. The light went out.

"It's me . . . Andy."

The light came back on, and Tug stepped forward. Andy could see the gleam of his eyes. "What are you following me for? Sneaking up on me like that?"

"I didn't follow you. I thought you were working on something. You know . . . something against the cops. I was thinking . . . do you think we could find a crab and put it in McGee's sleeping bag?"

Andy moved a little. Now he could see into the hole. Something square and white gleamed against the dark sand.

"Well, I'm not working on anything. Not right now. Go on back."

Andy bit his lip. Something told him to do just that. But something else made him want to know what was happening.

"What have you got in the hole?"

"I said, go on back."

Andy didn't move.

"Why don't you yell for your friend McGee?" Tug asked.

"Come on!" Andy said. "You know how much I hate him."

Tug stood very still. Then suddenly he picked up something and tossed it to Andy.

It was a Band-Aid tin, and it rattled.

Andy opened the lid. He tipped the box in his hand. A watch slid out, and some cuff links. There was the gleam of gold and a rich, red glow.

"Rubies," Tug said softly.

Andy slid the watch and cuff links back into the box. His hand felt hot. "The banker's?"

"Mine," Tug said. "They were the banker's." He knelt and put the tin back in the hole. Carefully he scraped sand over it.

"Will you . . . be able to find it again?"

"Sure." Tug tramped the sand flat. "This rock has two points, like rabbit ears."

"Oh." Andy's thoughts were a jumble as they walked back. "Some day Tug will get in bad trouble." How many times had his mom said that? Stealing was bad trouble, all right.

"You had better find a way to give them back," he said.

"Are you kidding?" Tug threw sand like a snowball. "There's at least 200 bucks' worth there. It was easy as pie. I just forced a drawer in the old guy's cabin. Skip always said ripping things off was easy as pie."

Andy felt a little sick. Had Skip said that? "Mr. Saunders will know one of the camp kids stole them," he said.

"Yeah. But which one? He's got 15 problem boys to choose from. Anyway, he won't miss them for a while. He hardly ever uses the boat.

One of the crew said so."

Andy could see the campfire and the shadows around it. He wished he had never left it.

"Too bad we have McGee in our tent," Tug said. "The stuff would have been safe in my backpack. But cops are just too nosy. You can't trust them."

Fergus looked up as they edged in by the fire. "Where have you two been?"

Tug opened his eyes wide. "Don't cops ever have to go to the bathroom?"

The boys rejoined the circle. Tug lay back and grinned. Andy felt all tight inside. *I know about it,* he thought. *That makes me part of it. They would pin it on me now as easily as Tug.*

CHAPTER 5

Andy learned a lot that week. He learned to snorkel. He learned how to climb a cliff. Everyone had to take a survival class after lunch from Charlie-O. They learned how to make wilderness shelters and distress signals.

"That will help when I'm lost at the North Pole," Tug said.

Charlie-O showed them the North Star in the night sky. "That one star has saved more lives than any other," he said. "It shows you which way is north."

"So what?" Tug said. "I'll look for it if I'm lost in the Sahara." Tug never cared that Charlie-O heard. But Charlie-O paid no attention. That seemed to bother Tug more than anything else.

They learned how to make splints. They learned what to do for snake bites.

"What about lion bites?" Tug asked. "I'm thinking about a trip to the zoo."

There was one thing Tug did take seriously. That was cliff climbing. McGee was the teacher.

Andy found cliff climbing hard. McGee showed them how to rappel. You put the rope around a tree so the ends hung down. Then you put the rope ends between your legs. You wrapped the rope around one thigh. Then it went over your chest, over your shoulder, across your back. You held the rope in one hand and slid down. Your feet walked you down the cliff

side. It was the scariest thing Andy had ever done.

McGee shouted down to him from above. "You can't fall as long as you hold on to the rope."

Andy felt like a fly on a wall. The cliff was so steep. The ground was so far away. He couldn't breathe. He couldn't move.

"Keep walking, Andy. Let the rope out as you go." McGee egged him on. Somehow he got down. The kids who had gone before him clapped. He was so dizzy his legs folded.

"Who wants to try it again?" McGee yelled. His eyes rested on Andy. "No one has to," he added. "But knowing how to do it could save your life sometime. Or someone else's."

"Yeah, when we're on Mount Everest," Tug said. But he climbed up cheerfully and rappelled down again.

"I really like that," he told Andy. "McGee teaching me how to be a second-story man."

"What's that?" Peewee asked.

"A cat burglar, dummy." Tug made crawling, spidery movements with his hands. He grinned at Andy. "The judge will ask, 'How did you learn to climb like that, Mr. Cat Burglar?' And I will say that I learned it at police camp!" Tug shouted with laughter.

Andy wasn't sure Tug was kidding. He had taken the banker's stuff He had gone over the borderline already.

27

For Andy, snorkeling was the best thing of all. Each day they took the dinghy to the reef and tied it up. Then they put on their masks, snorkels, and fins. Fergus taught them to breathe through the tube. He showed them a way to kick without getting tired.

It was another world under the water. All kinds of sea creatures clung to the reef. Colored fish brushed against them as they swam. Andy felt as if he were one of them.

Fergus had thrown Tug out of the class the first day. Tug had yelled, "Shark! Shark!" All the kids had tried frantically to climb into the dinghy. It had almost capsized. Tug had just about died laughing. Andy had never seen anyone as mad as Fergus.

"We don't fool about things like that," he said. "Do you know what your problem is? You don't care about anyone, Tug. You spoil things for yourself and people around you. I don't want you in my class."

Andy tried to be sorry. But he wasn't. It wasn't fun snorkeling with Tug. You never knew what he'd do.

"I never should have touched that stuff on the way over," Tug said one night. "I should have waited till we were going back."

"Did you ever think you never should have touched it at all?"

"This is risky," Tug went on. "It's dumb to take

that kind of risk. Look what happened to Skip."

Andy bit his fingernail. "You knew all along Skip took that purse, didn't you?"

"Sure," Tug said. "They found it in your bushes, didn't they? Skip's fingerprints were all over it."

"He said it was empty when he found it."

"But you knew he took it too, didn't you?" Tug asked.

"Yeah," Andy said slowly. "I guess I did."

Tug's eyes gazed over Andy's head. "What if the old banker guy did use his boat this week? What if they search us on the way back?" He was talking to himself, thinking. "I know. I could plant it on someone. I'd take it from him when we got off." He smiled at Andy. "Yeah! Peewee Peters! No one would suspect him."

"You're kidding, Tug," Andy said. "Even you wouldn't do a thing like that."

But he knew Tug would. That was something else he'd learned that week. It was like snorkeling. Without the mask on, everything was hazy. With it, things were sharp and clear.

Now he saw Tug through the mask. And Skip too. And even himself.

"No," Tug said. "Peewee is such a cry baby. If he found the stuff, he'd yell for McGee. I'll find a better way."

But in the end, Tug didn't even have to look for a better way. McGee gave it to him.

CHAPTER 6

McGee liked to talk before he went to sleep. Tug gave him smart-mouth answers; Andy just listened. McGee said a lot of neat things. He told them about a tribe in Africa that had never seen white men. He told about someone who had found King Solomon's mines. He talked about all kinds of stuff.

On the last night, Andy lay all tensed up in his sleeping bag. He could hear the sea murmuring aginst the cliffs. He thought of the Los Angeles streets, and of vacant lots with their dirty city weeds. He didn't want to go back.

"Will there be camp next year?" he asked. He saw the blur that was McGee's face.

"I hope so, Andy. If we can get funding. And, if Mr. Saunders lends his boat again."

"That Mr. Saunders sure is a good guy," Tug said.

Andy felt a sting of tears. "Shut up, Tug," he said. He felt like getting out of the sleeping bag and kicking Tug. Tug knew the banker wouldn't lend the boat next year. Not to a bunch of thieves. "You spoil things for yourself and people around you," Fergus had said. Fergus was right.

"Shut up yourself." There were all kinds of warnings in Tug's voice. But it got soft and slippery as he spoke to McGee. "I bet you won't ask me back next year."

"Sure we will," McGee said.

"I'm sorry it's over." Andy stuffed the corner of the sleeping bag into his mouth. Why had he said that? He couldn't let McGee inside his head that way. McGee, who had sent Skip to Juvenile Hall. Skip, who really had stolen that purse — and others. But still . . .

"Listen!" McGee raised himself on one elbow. "I'm not going back on the boat tomorrow. I'm hiking across the island. I'll spend an overnight. Then I'll take the steamer from port the next day. Do you want to come with me, Andy?" McGee asked.

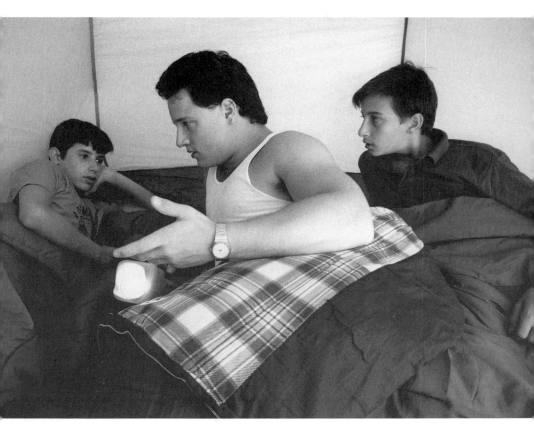

Andy pulled the sleeping bag over his chin.

"It's a long walk," McGee said. "And there's a cliff to climb." McGee hesitated. "It's not steep. And there are no cliffs to go down."

"I'll go," Tug said loudly.

McGee was silent.

"Or is it just Andy you want?" Tug managed to sound really hurt.

Oh wow, Andy thought. He could hear the wheels turning in Tug's head. This way he'd miss the power boat. He'd miss the search if there was one. He'd walk out with the stuff, easy as pie!

"You can come if you want, Tug. What do you say, Andy?" McGee asked.

Andy lay very still. Another day. One last adventure. With McGee, though — and Tug. The thought of Tug was bad now. *Tug has changed,* he thought. *Or maybe I've changed.*

"Well, Andy?"

"OK," Andy said.

"Great! Fergus can call your mothers. You'll be a day late." McGee sighed and squirmed down.

Andy slept and then awoke to a small sound. Tug was crawling out of the tent. Later he heard him come back. *He's all set,* Andy thought. *He's got his stuff and it was easy as pie.*

McGee made Tug and Andy do their share of breaking camp before they left.

Tug kept looking to see if the power boat was in sight. "Come on. Let's get going," he urged.

McGee set out everything they would need. They divided it between the three packs.

Tug jammed his share in his backpack. "Let's move," he said.

McGee hung the coil of rope over Andy's shoulder.

They were ready. They yelled their good-byes and began walking.

Soon the sound of the sea got fainter. Birds rose from the long grass under their feet.

"California quail," McGee said. Those were the only words anyone spoke till they came to a river.

McGee stopped. "It's running shallow," he said. "We'll have no trouble."

The river ran brown and fast. Mossy rocks dotted it, like stepping stones. McGee went first. Then Andy. Tug was almost across when he slipped. He half sat, then sprawled in the water. McGee held out a hand and Tug grabbed it.

McGee grinned. "That will cool you off."

Tug squeezed water from his shirt.

"Here," McGee said. "Give me your pack." He eased it from Tug's shoulders. "Your sleeping bag is wet too. You had better unroll it. Your stuff can dry while we wait."

A stream of water ran from the backpack. McGee opened the buckle. "No," Tug whispered. He jumped forward. But it was too late.

McGee had upended the pack on the river bank. Everything tumbled out. Andy saw the white shine of the Band-Aid tin. Then the lid sprang open. The ruby cuff links winked like two red eyes.

CHAPTER 7

Andy saw everything in slow motion.

McGee picked up the cuff links. The watch had slid half out of the tin. McGee turned it over. "J.S.," he read aloud.

Tug grabbed his arm but McGee held the things out of reach.

"Those are mine," Tug yelled.

"I don't think so."

McGee's face was a cop face again. The way it had been back at the station house. The way it had been when he came for Skip.

"J.S.," McGee said. "John Saunders." His glance moved from Tug to Andy. "Did you have any part in this, Andy?"

"No," Andy said. "I knew Tug had done it. Afterward. But I couldn't tell you."

"It's OK, Andy." McGee's voice was gentle.

Andy looked at him and he knew what he really had known always. McGee was all right. There was no use blaming him because Skip wasn't . . . or Tug wasn't . . . or he wasn't . . .

Andy watched McGee put the stuff back in the tin. The lid snapped shut. McGee took off his own pack and put the tin inside.

"He shouldn't leave things like that lying around," Tug said. "That's asking to have them taken."

"Don't give me that, Tug. You searched pretty well before you found these." McGee sounded

36

tired. "We'll go see him and give them back. With luck he won't press charges."

"What do you mean with luck? I'm not going anywhere. I'm not telling him anything." Tug was shaking. "Heck, I never saw those things before. Somebody must have put them in my pack. One of those rotten kids." His eyes darted to Andy. "Hey, Andy? Didn't you say you saw Peewee Peters sneaking around our tent today?"

"No, I didn't," Andy said.

McGee rubbed his eyes. "Spread your wet

stuff out, Tug. We'd better eat."

They ate standing. They had cold beans and franks, straight from the can. When he finished, Tug hurled his empty can away.

"Pick that up," McGee said sharply. "This island isn't a garbage dump." McGee put his in his pack. "And put your gear back. We have to get moving."

"It's still wet," Tug muttered.

"Tough," McGee said.

Now Andy led. Tug was in the middle and McGee walked last. From time to time McGee checked his compass.

"Turn left, Andy. Hold it. Make for that rock over there."

Tug hummed and kicked at the long grass.

What would McGee do if Tug made a run for it? Did McGee have a gun? No, not at camp. What if Tug jumped him? Tug was pretty strong.

"Andy?" The whisper was warm on his neck. "We'll rush him. When I whistle . . ."

"Drop back, Tug," McGee said. "Save your breath for walking. Move it faster, Andy. It's up to you to set the pace."

About 10 minutes went by. Tug whispered again. "He put Skip away. Remember?"

Remember Skip. Remember Mom saying, "I've cried over one son." "No," Andy said out loud.

"Hold up!" McGee said. He had the compass out. "That's the cliff we have to go up. It's an

easy climb by that ridge. It's loose shale but not too steep. Just remember to test every hold before you put your weight on it."

It wasn't steep where they climbed. But there were sheer drop-offs. Andy tried not to look at them as they went up. What if your foot slipped? What if you rolled right over the edge? Shale rattled under his feet.

"Watch it!" Tug yelled angrily. "That stuff is

clobbering me, for Pete's sake!"

"I'm trying to watch it," Andy muttered. They were three quarters of the way up now. A mountain sheep watched them curiously from another ridge.

They were almost to the top now. It hadn't been bad. There was a football-sized rock within reach. Andy stretched for it. The rock pulled out of the ground as he put his weight on it. He grabbed a tuft of coarse grass.

"Tug!" Andy yelled. The rock rolled and bounced. Tug saw it coming and swung himself to the side. The rock slammed into McGee's shoulder. There was a kind of dull thump.

McGee crumpled as if his legs had melted. His hands opened. He and the rock bounced together. McGee fell over the edge.

The sliding noise stopped. The world was filled with the worst silence Andy had ever heard. Above the pounding of his heart was a sharp, clicking sound. It was the mountain sheep, hightailing it away.

Somehow Andy got himself to the top. Behind him he heard Tug's gasps and grunts. They were up now, standing in the long grass of a high field. Andy forced himself to walk to the cliff edge and look over. McGee was down there — way, way down. He lay on his back on a ledge. He wasn't moving.

Tug pushed Andy aside. He peered down,

then turned to Andy. Tug's face was a strange gray color. "Do you think he's dead?" he asked.

"I . . . I . . ." Andy couldn't get words past the tightness in his throat.

"No sweat," Tug said slowly. "It was an accident. But man, it sure is some break for me! We'll keep going. Then we can tell somebody. No one is going to blame us."

"You mean . . . leave him here?"

"What else?" Tug wasn't so gray anymore. "Do you want to go down that cliff? What good would it do if he's dead?"

"Maybe he isn't," Andy said.

"Yeah. Maybe he isn't."

Andy stared at Tug and Tug looked away. But Andy had seen his eyes and he knew what Tug hoped. And knowing what Tug hoped was the scariest thing of all.

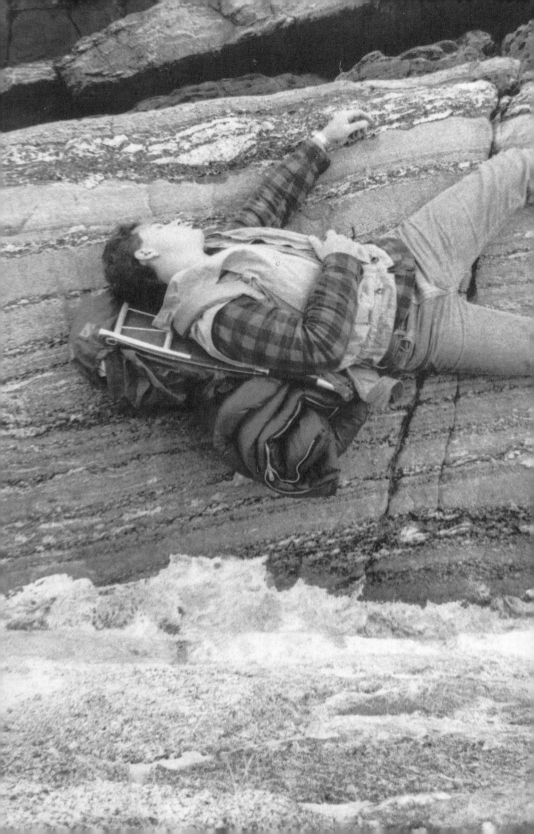

CHAPTER 8

"Do you think we can find our way?" Tug asked. "Without a compass?"

"I don't know." Andy clenched his hands in his pockets. If only he could stop shaking. "We've got to find out if he's alive, Tug. We've got to."

"I don't 'got to' do anything," Tug said.

"Well, I've got to," Andy said.

"You mean . . . " Tug did the crawly spidery thing with his hands. "You mean, go down?"

Andy nodded. "Don't think about that smooth wall of rock," he told himself. "Don't think about hanging from a rope with nothing but space underneath. Don't think about the way you swing away from the side."

Tug walked to the cliff edge. "Well," he said, "he hasn't moved. When you're down there, don't forget to bring up the compass and . . ."

Andy watched the thoughts flicker across Tug's face. He was remembering that Band-Aid tin in McGee's pack.

Tug glanced at Andy through narrowed eyes. "I'm better on the rope than you are," he said. "Give it to me. I'll go." He slipped off his pack and sleeping bag.

Andy turned the coil round and round in his hands. There was a terrible relief in him that Tug would go. But still . . . "It should be me," he said.

Tug grinned. "You'd never make it, kid." Tug

took the rope and looped it around a tree. He yanked the ends, testing. "Between your legs. Around your thigh. Across your chest. Over your shoulder. Down your back." Tug muttered the words as he fixed the rope. "OK. Here goes."

For a second Andy saw Tug hang out over the cliff edge. Then he was sliding down. Andy lay on his stomach and peered over. Even watching made him dizzy.

Slowly, slowly, Tug cliff-walked closer to the ledge. Now he was down. He unwrapped the rope and knelt beside McGee.

Andy cupped his hands around his mouth. "Is he alive?" he shouted.

Tug started to jerk the backpack out from under McGee.

"Be careful!" Andy yelled. "If he's hurt you

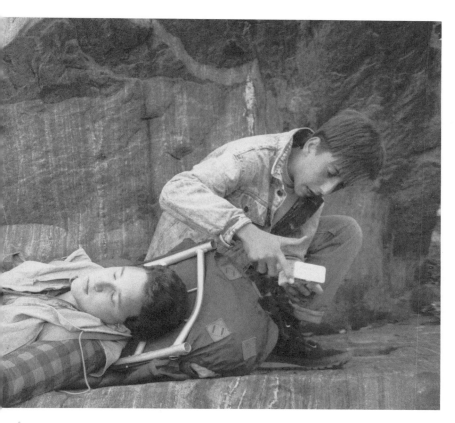

shouldn't move him."

Tug took the Band-Aid tin from McGee's pack. He took the compass from McGee's jacket pocket.

Andy turned the side of his face to the grass. *McGee's dead*, he thought, *and I did it.*

Tug was climbing back up. He pulled himself up the rope hand over hand. His toes found holds that Andy couldn't see. He hauled himself over the top and grinned. "Easy as pie."

Andy's throat had closed again. "Is he dead?" he croaked.

Tug was pulling the rope back up. The silence lay like mist between them.

"Tug!" Andy was shouting now. He grabbed Tug's arm. "Is he dead? Why won't you answer me?"

"Because I don't know. I couldn't tell."

"You could too. He's not dead. That's it, isn't it? You won't tell me because then I won't leave. You want him to be dead so you can keep that lousy . . ."

Andy jumped on Tug. They rolled together, close to the cliff edge. Tug broke away. They stood, facing each other, panting.

"Are you crazy?" Tug gasped. "I didn't brain him with that rock. You did. And I don't care if

you leave or not. All I know is, I'm going." He picked up his pack and sleeping bag. He took the compass from his pocket and studied it. "What's it going to be, Andy?"

What's it going to be, Andy? He could just walk away with Tug. No sweat. No hassle. No cliff. It was his choice. Dimly he knew, somehow, that it was the biggest choice of his life.

"Well?" Tug asked.

Andy wet his lips. "I'm staying."

"You're stupid," Tug said flatly.

"Will you . . . will you send help?"

"Sure." Tug's face told Andy nothing.

Andy watched him go. He watched till Tug was small in the distance. Then he knew there

was no way to put it off any longer.

He checked McGee. McGee was still there. Of course he was still there. Andy checked the rope. It was still there too. Its ends dangled down the cliff. Tug had dropped them when Andy jumped him. There was no way to put it off any longer. He took off his pack and sleeping bag.

"Between your legs. Around your thigh." He knew it too.

Now he was going over the edge.

"Keep your feet spread. Brace them against the cliff." In his mind, Andy heard McGee's voice.

"Keep walking, Andy. Don't stop."

The rope burned his hands. He was letting it out too fast. Slow down. Don't panic. His feet scrambled for a hold, slipped, stuck again.

"You can't fall if you hold on to the rope." Can't fall. Something rattled. Were there snakes? Don't panic.

The ledge. He was down. He crouched, afraid to let go of the rope. He could stand here. The ledge was wide enough so there was no need to be scared of falling off.

He let the rope go and stood with his back to the cliff. Beyond the ledge, the world dropped off to nothingness. And there, almost at the edge, was McGee.

Andy dropped to his hands and knees beside the cop.

CHAPTER 9

The ledge was bigger than it looked from above. But it sloped to a fall-off. Dry bushes edged the base of the cliff in places. Some clung to the cliff walls.

McGee lay with his shoulders and head on the backpack. It was the way Tug had left him. Brush had cushioned his fall and stopped him from rolling farther. His eyes were closed.

Andy touched his face. It was warm. He bent over and put his ear to McGee's chest. Nothing. A pulse . . . that was what he needed to find. He lifted McGee's wrist. A pulse beat under his fingers.

Andy sat back on his heels and closed his eyes. McGee was alive. He hadn't killed him

after all. McGee was alive.

He got the pack and sleeping bag off McGee's shoulders. They had kept him propped up. Now he rolled onto his back. Andy gritted his teeth. *Sorry, McGee. I'll be careful.* He took off his own jacket and put it under McGee's head.

Right away he felt the chill. It would be cold soon. Here on the ledge there would be no shelter.

He wondered how bad McGee was. One of his legs looked kind of funny. Andy touched it gently. It was bent the wrong way. Should he straighten it? He decided to leave it alone.

He unrolled the sleeping bag and spread it over McGee. What else should he do?

He pulled everything from McGee's pack.

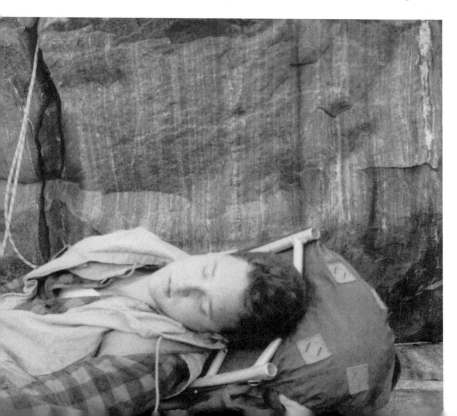

There was a sweat shirt and extra socks. McGee's knife in its sheath. A can of beef stew. The empty can from lunch. A small first aid kit. A can opener. Matches. A flashlight. A plastic sheet. A plastic bag had twigs for starting a fire. A canteen was half full of water.

Andy put the sweat shirt on. He tried to think what was in his pack . . . the pack he'd left up on top of the cliff. Too late now to know he should have let the pack and sleeping bag down first. He hadn't. And he sure wasn't going back up to get them now. Tomorrow he'd have to . . . if someone didn't find them tonight.

The sun was lower now. It would be dark soon. Dark and cold. No one would find them before tomorrow. He wouldn't think past tomorrow.

"Andy!"

Andy almost jumped out of his skin. McGee! McGee was talking! Andy crawled over to him. McGee's eyes were dazed. "What . . .?"

"It's OK," Andy said quickly. "You fell. We're on a ledge. Tug's gone for help."

"Leg," McGee said. His tongue came out to touch his lips.

"You want water?" Andy crawled as fast as he could to the canteen. When he brought it back, McGee's eyes were closed again. "McGee?" Andy whispered. There was no answer.

Fear came in a rush. Andy grabbed McGee's

wrist. The pulse beat was as steady as a clock ticking. He looked at McGee's face. He had never liked the dimple in McGee's cheek. It was dumb-looking. His hair was fine, like a baby's! Andy felt his throat burn, and there was hurting behind his eyes. *Don't die,* he begged silently. *Just don't die.*

The sun was disappearing. He had to hurry.

He crawled around the ledge getting dry brush. Small pine needles had fallen from above. He found an old bird's nest in some bushes. Soon he had a small pile.

Then, with McGee's knife, he cut at the bushes. His pile grew. It was almost dark. As he cut brush by the cliff, he found an overhang. It was crawl-space size. He remembered the rattling he had heard earlier and looked around. No sign of snakes.

It was hard to see. McGee's shape was only a long shadow. Where should he have the fire? He studied the ledge. That was when McGee moved.

Andy heard the sound of shale falling. McGee was trying to sit up.

Andy's heart seemed to stop. "McGee! McGee, stay still!" he yelled.

McGee was pushing aside the sleeping bag. He was turning toward the cliff edge.

Andy flung himself forward. His hands caught McGee's shoulders. He pushed him down.

McGee's scream of pain echoed in space.

"I'm sorry. I'm sorry, McGee. Did I knock your leg? I'm sorry."

But McGee was out again. His face was turned to the darkness of the sky.

Sweat rolled down Andy's back. That was something he hadn't thought of. He couldn't leave McGee this close to the edge. What if he rolled over? But you shouldn't move someone with a broken leg. Not unless it was splinted or something. Well, he had to move him. One risk was worse than the other.

He took away the sleeping bag and jacket. Inch by inch he dragged McGee back to the crawl space. "Almost there," he panted. "Hold on, McGee." And he felt each jolt even though McGee couldn't.

McGee's leg didn't seem to be part of him. It slithered to the side of him like a small animal.

Andy got him into the shelter. He made the pillow again and covered him.

Now he had to use the flashlight to see.

He piled the brush between the crawl space and the cliff edge. It would be a fire barrier.

The dry nest caught fire at once. Andy pushed it under the pile. Good. He'd have the fire-starting twigs for next time.

Flames darted, orange and yellow. The brush crackled and snapped. Andy dozed off and on. He tucked the sheet of plastic around them both.

He put on McGee's extra socks. From time to time he added to the fire.

Once he felt McGee's forehead. It was burning hot. There were aspirin in the first aid kit. He mashed two with water. But the mixture trickled from McGee's mouth over his chin.

The North Star was high in the night sky. Andy kept his eyes on it. Was Tug walking through the night? Would help come soon . . . soon enough for McGee?

Andy shivered. He wouldn't want to bet on it.

CHAPTER 10

When Andy woke up, the fire was out.

He felt McGee's face. It seemed even hotter. "McGee?" he whispered.

McGee didn't wake up.

Their ledge was out of the morning sun. It was cold.

Andy decided not to start another fire. He had to save what brush they had. What if he heard a plane? He'd need the smoke for a signal.

He tried to figure out how soon help would come. If Tug had walked all night, he'd be at the town by now. Any minute Andy might hear voices calling, or the drone of a search plane.

But no one came.

The sun was hot when it reached the ledge. Heat shimmered and bounced off the cliff. Andy took the sleeping bag off McGee.

McGee was restless. Once he muttered, "Charlie-O." Once he asked for water. Again it ran from his mouth. Andy wet one of the socks. He wiped McGee's face and hands.

The sun was burning down on McGee's face. Andy took off the sweat shirt and hung it where it shaded McGee's head.

He ate the can of stew. Slowly he swallowed all but the last sip of water in the canteen. He sat against the cliff, trying to think things out.

It must be mid-afternoon. No one had come. What if Tug hadn't told anyone? Andy had to face that possibility. When he and Tug didn't come home tonight, their mothers would check with the police station. They'd raise the alarm. But that would be tonight. Searchers wouldn't come at night. Figure tomorrow morning. What if he went for help himself? Would it get here faster? Thoughts swished around in his head. Yet it felt empty, like the canteen.

Andy shook his head to clear it. He had to stay with McGee. At least until . . . until what? Until tomorrow? Until McGee died?

They needed water. He looked at the rope. "Going up isn't so bad," he told himself. "Forget about coming back down."

"Don't worry, McGee," he said out loud. "I'll be back."

Andy grabbed the rope. He was about halfway up when he heard the sound. He swung on the rope, afraid to move. The helicopter passed right overhead. "Here! Here!" Andy screamed. His voice was as shrill as a bird's.

The helicopter shadow crawled like a huge spider on the gully floor. Andy burned his hands on the rope coming down. The helicopter disappeared over the next ridge.

Andy stood waving the sweat shirt. "Come back! Come back!" he yelled. But the motor sound faded into silence.

He knelt on the ledge and fought the need to cry. Don't cry, dummy. Think! They'll be back.

59

They're searching for us. Of course they're searching for us.

He crept around getting a fire ready. At the first sound of the motor, he'd light it.

Once he thought he heard it coming back. His hands shook so badly that he could hardly get the match lit. But he did it. Then he found he had only imagined the sound of a helicopter. And he had to let the fire burn itself out.

Time passed slowly. The sun was red and sinking. Andy didn't mean to sleep, but he did. Through his dream he heard the helicopter come back. He opened dazed eyes and looked at the sky.

There it was, hovering two ridges away. He was sobbing as he fumbled for the matches. The fire was going. But it would be too late. Because he had slept. Because he had slept!

The sun was in his eyes. The sun! The empty can. The shiny can lid! Charlie-O! Signals. The lid!

Andy grabbed it and held it to the sun. He moved it back and forth. "Please," he whispered.

The helicopter moved on. "Turn and look. Please! Please!"

Had it slowed down? It had. It was turning, coming back, hovering above them.

Andy shaded his eyes. A man with a megaphone stood in the open side of the helicopter.

"We're letting down a vest. Can you put it on the injured man? Wave if you can."

Andy waved.

He inched McGee out. McGee looked bad.

The vest came down on a cable. Andy put it on McGee. A safety lock clicked. He tried to ease McGee's leg as he was lifted.

McGee dangled in the air. Slowly, he was drawn up. Hands pulled him into the helicopter.

Then it was Andy's turn.

Up, up, up.

The ledge was a small shelf. Mountains and valleys turned below him. He saw the sea.

Someone helped him over the helicopter's edge. Someone unbuckled his vest. His legs melted and he sat down.

The noise was deafening. McGee lay on a

stretcher in back. A man stood beside him. Andy made his way to them. "Will . . . will he die?" he shouted.

"Naw," the man yelled. "I don't like the look of that leg, but he's far from dying. What were you two doing out there anyway?"

Andy felt as if he were floating outside himself. "We were at camp all week," he said. "McGee and I were hiking."

"Y camp?"

"Cop camp," Andy said. "So kids and cops could get to know each other better."

The man grinned. "Did it work?"

"It worked." Andy paused. "You were looking for us, weren't you?"

The man shook his head. "Uh-uh! Somebody saw a fire up on the ridge last night. He called it in this morning. But we couldn't find anything. We were ready to give up when we saw your signal."

"Oh." So Tug hadn't sent them. Andy felt a stab of disappointment, but he wasn't really surprised. Tug was over the borderline. There was no sense in pretending he wasn't.

Andy sat in a seat and closed his eyes. "At least McGee and I are safe," he said to himself. "That's the most important thing."

But his mind drifted back to Tug. Crossing over the borderline was easy as pie. He wondered how hard it was to cross back.